The Kitten with no Name

Vivian French

Illustrated by
Selina Young

Orion
Children's Books

To dearest Nat,
love from Gumble

X X

The Kitten With No Name originally
appeared in *The Story House*
first published in Great Britain in 2004
by Orion Children's Books
This edition first published in 2011
by Orion Children's Books
a division of the Orion Publishing Group Ltd
Orion House
5 Upper St Martin's Lane
London WC2H 9EA
An Hachette UK Company

Designed by Louise Millar

A catalogue record for this book
is available from the British Library

Printed and bound in China

ISBN 978 1 4440 0078 8

Contents

Chapter One

Once there was a kitten without a name. He was born under a hedge, so he had no home either.

"MeeOW," said his mother. "When you are big enough I'll take you somewhere very special where we can live happily ever after."

"Why is it special?" asked the kitten.

"Well," said his mother, "because it'll be our very own home."

"Our own home!" the kitten said.

"That sounds good. But how will we know when we've found the right place?"
His mother began to purr.
"We'll know," she said. "We'll feel warm and cosy and someone will love us."
The kitten snuggled down against his mother's soft fur.
"That's the best bit," said the kitten and he began to purr.

"Purr ... purr ... purr."

Every day the kitten with no name scrambled out from under the hedge to play with the waving buttercups and catch the dancing daisies and chase the butterflies that went flying past.

"Don't go too far," said his mother.
"I won't," said the kitten.

One day the kitten found an old conker. He patted it and it bounced across the ground.

The kitten ran after it – straight into a group of children.

"Oh!" said a tall boy. "Look! What a pretty kitten!" He picked the kitten up and hugged him.

"H'm," thought the kitten.
"Being hugged is good. I've never been hugged before."

"Purr ... purr ... purr."

"Want to see the kitty," said a very little girl. "Pretty kitty. Take him home?"

"No, Daisy B," said the tall boy. "We've already got Fat Freda and Big Tom and Kitty Purr too – there's no room for another cat. Come on, let's go to the park. I'll push you on the swings."

"Yes!" shouted the very little girl.
"Bye bye, pretty kitty.
See you soon."

The kitten ran back to his mother
under the hedge.

"Mother," he said. "I was hugged!"

"Hugging is good if it isn't too tight," said his mother.

"It wasn't too tight," the kitten said. "It was nice. And a little girl wanted to take me home!"

His mother jumped to her feet
"You must **never** let anyone take
you home," she said. "We're going
to go to our own home!"

The kitten looked hopeful.
"Will we be hugged?"
"Of course," said his mother.
"Now wash your paws and whiskers
and I'll tuck you up."

The kitten curled up in his little leafy bed. "I think," he said sleepily, "I shall dream about being hugged." And he shut his eyes and began to purr.

Chapter Two

One day the kitten who had no name
was chasing a big white butterfly,
when he heard his mother calling him.

"Be a good kitten," she said, "and stay by our hedge. I'm going to the end of the field to see what I can see."

"Are you going to find our special place where we can live happily for ever and ever?" asked the kitten hopefully.

"Not today," said his mother. "I'm just going to see how the weather will be tomorrow."

The kitten watched the big white butterfly fly out of reach and then he sat down to think.

"If Mother sees that I'm big enough to go to the end of the field, she'll see that I'm big enough to go with her and find our new home. And maybe—" the kitten jumped up "—we could go today!"

And off he went.

The grass in the field was long and thick.

"MeeOW, I can't see where to go," he said.

He jumped
and he bounded
and he leapt.

And he leapt
and he bounded
and he jumped.

And he bounded
and he leapt
and he jumped.

And he bounded.

And he stopped.

"I'm tired," said the kitten.
His paws hurt and there was
grass seed in his fur.
"I think I'll go back now."

"Which way do I go?"
he thought. "Is it this way?"

But it wasn't.

"Is it that way?" he wondered.

But it wasn't.

"It must be this way," said the kitten.

But it wasn't.

"Oh dear," said the kitten and
he sat down under a large thistle.
"I think I'm lost."

Chapter Three

Two big tears rolled down the
kitten's nose.
There was a rustling in the grass
and a squeaking.

The kitten sniffed loudly.
"Mother?"

A mouse popped her head from out under a thistle leaf. "Oh my best whiskers!" she said. "It's a kitten!"

"Hello," the kitten said. "Have you seen my mother?"

"No," said the mouse. She looked around nervously. "Is she near?"

"I don't know," said the kitten. "I'm lost."

"Oh." The mouse sat down beside him. "Where do you live?"

"Under a big hedge," said the kitten.

"A big hedge?" said the mouse. "That's easy. You see that yellow gorse bush over there?"

The kitten looked. "Yes," he said.

"The big hedge is just a step and a hop further on," said the mouse, and she skipped away.

"Thank you!" said the kitten
and he began jumping ...

and bounding ...

and leaping ...

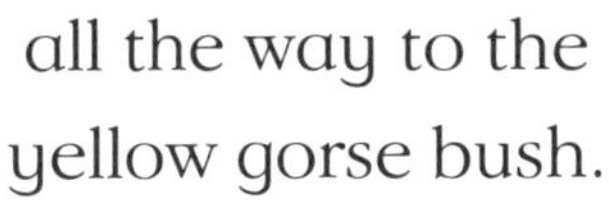

all the way to the
yellow gorse bush.

"I'll soon be back now," said the kitten."But I'm very tired. Maybe I'll have a little sleep. Mother won't be there just yet."

He curled himself into a neat little ball, and began to dream of a very special place covered in pretty yellow flowers … a warm and cosy place to live in for ever and ever.

Chapter Four

The kitten who had no name slept and slept. When he woke up it was getting late.

He looked about and there,
sure enough, was a big hedge.
It wasn't far away at all.

"I'd better hurry," said the kitten.
He ran with a hop and a skip and a
jump and he didn't look
where he was going.

Splash

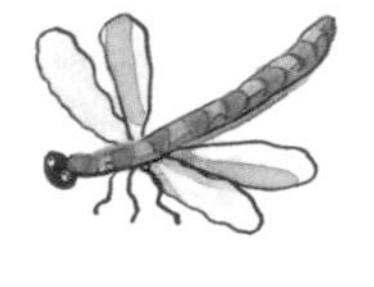

The kitten fell into a stream.

"Meeeeow!" he shrieked.

"Meeeeow!

Mother! Mother!

Meeeeow!"

Down and down he sank and then
up and up he bobbed again.

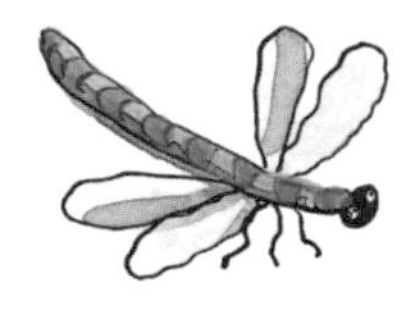

Down and down …

"Flip my flippers," said
a croaky voice.

Someone or something seized
the kitten by the scruff of the neck.
Someone or something pulled him
out of the stream.

"Flip my flippers and what have
we got here?"
The kitten opened his eyes.
A large green frog was standing
in front of him. "You should learn to
swim, young animal," said the frog.

He began to rub the kitten's wet fur
with a handful of grass.
"Not that it wasn't a good jump.
Not as good as us frogs do, of course,
but not bad at all."

The frog suddenly stopped.
"Dear me! Are you meant to be furry?"
The kitten nodded.

"That's all right, then." The frog went on rubbing. "I wondered if the water had done something funny to your scales. Or your feathers."

He gave the kitten a final pat.
"Go on, then. Tell us what you are."

"I'm a kitten," said the kitten.
"I was trying to get back to my mother,
but the stream got in the way."
And he began to cry.
"Now now now," said the frog.
"Tears never sorted anything.
What we need is action!"
"Do we?" asked the kitten.

The frog nodded. "You curl up here by the dandelions. I'll go and get my friend. He'll take you over the stream – no trouble."

The kitten yawned. He did feel tired and the sun felt warm and comfortable on his back.

"Thank you very much," he said. "Will your friend really help me?"

"Sure as tadpoles turn into frogs," said the frog. He jumped back into the stream with a plop!

The kitten yawned again.
"I'll soon be back with my mother,"
he thought. "And then we can find
our special place … and someone
there will love us and hug us …"
And he drifted off to sleep.

Chapter Five

"Quack!" The kitten woke up with a start. A duck was standing beside him.

"**Quack!**" said the duck. "Are you a kitten?"

The kitten nodded.

"Good," said the duck. "Frog says you need to cross the stream."

"Oh yes, please!" said the kitten.

There was a loud splash, and Frog came leaping up the bank. "Kitten," he said, "this is Duck. Duck, my friend, can you take this young fellow over the stream? "

"I live under the big green hedge," the kitten said. "Can you really take me over the stream?"

The duck thought for a moment. "If he sat on a lily leaf we could push it across."

"Flip my flippers!" said the frog. "What a brain! Two ticks, and I'll be back."

He dived into the water, chose the biggest lily leaf, and swam over towing it behind him.

"Here you are, young fellow. Hop on!"

The kitten went nervously to the edge of the stream.

"OOOOOOOh!"

he said, as he felt the lily pad tremble underneath his paws.

"Try shutting your eyes," said the frog.

The kitten shut his eyes as the lily pad moved slowly across the stream.

"Nearly there!" said the frog.

He gave the lily pad a huge heave.

The lily pad wobbled.

"Meow!" The kitten held on as tightly as he could.

"Quack!" said the duck.

"Here we are!"

"Oh – meeeeeOW!"

The kitten jumped onto dry land,
"Thank you! Thank you!" he said.
"I'll never forget you!"
The frog and the duck waved as
the kitten hurried towards the
big green hedge.

"Mother!" the kitten
called. "Mother!
I'm here!"

The kitten scampered across the grass
– and then stopped.
It wasn't his hedge.
It was just like where he lived, but he
knew it was wrong. It was terribly wrong.
The kitten sat down and cried.
"Meow! Meow!"

"Sh!" said a voice.
"Sh! You'll wake my babies!"
The kitten spun round.
Behind him was a rabbit.

"I'm very sorry," said the kitten.
"I'm lost!"

"Lost?" The rabbit looked shocked.
"But you should be at home."
The kitten sighed. "I thought this
was my hedge, but it isn't."

"Silly little thing," said the rabbit.
"I expect you've wandered too far up.
Stay near the hedge and you'll find
your way." She disappeared into her
hole with a whisk of her white fluffy tail.

"Oh!" The kitten suddenly
felt much better.

Pop!

The rabbit was back. "A little thing like you shouldn't be out so late," she said. "Come along and stay the night here – but mind you tiptoe."

The kitten didn't argue. It was getting dark, and there were strange noises that made him shiver. He followed the rabbit, and found himself in a warm burrow filled with soft grass.

"There!" she said.

"Thank you," whispered the kitten, and he snuggled down in the grass.

Chapter Six

The kitten woke up feeling bright and cheerful. The three baby bunnies were still fast asleep, but Mother Rabbit was tidying up.

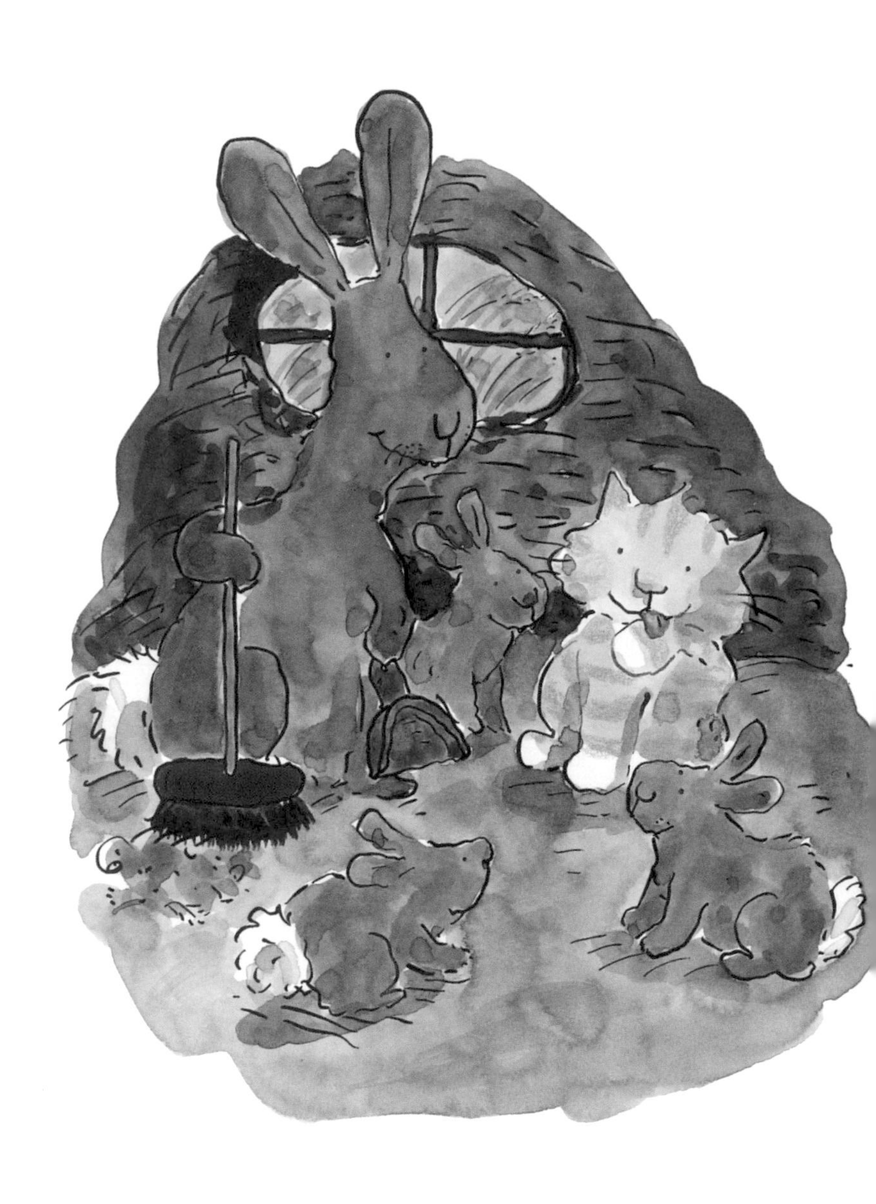

"There's a good little kitten," she said. "Now, come and have some breakfast, and then you must run along and find your mother. She'll be worried sick!"

The kitten nodded. "I'm ready!" he said. "And I'm hungry."

"That's good," said the rabbit, and she gave him a very small carrot.

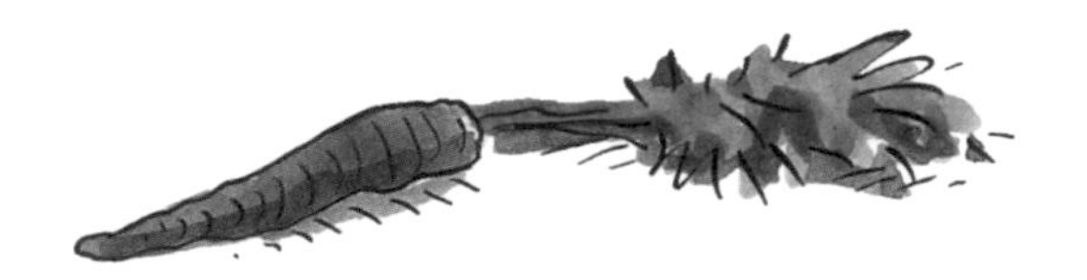

The kitten's whiskers drooped. "Oh," he said, as politely as he could. "Thank you." He tried hard to eat the carrot, but he didn't like it much.

"Time to run along," the rabbit said. "Follow the hedge and you're sure to find your way."

The kitten looked round the burrow. It felt very warm and cosy, and the world outside seemed very big.

"Now, now," said the rabbit, "you'll be fine."

"Yes," said the kitten. "And thank you for looking after me.

It was a chilly grey day. The kitten shivered, and then shook himself. "Won't Mother be pleased to see me! We can have breakfast together. **Mew!** I'm so hungry!"

And he began to hurry along, purring as he went.

"Cuckoo! Cuckoo!
Cuckoo!
Help me! Help!
Oh, won't anyone help me?"

The kitten froze.
The voice was coming from
above him, high up in the hedge.

"Please! Please help me!"

The kitten peered up
between the leaves.
A feather floated past
his nose, and he sneezed.

"AtchOOO!"

The kitten shook
the feather off.
"Meeow!
I'm coming!"
he called, and
he wriggled in
between the twigs
and the branches.
There wasn't
much room for
even a little
kitten.

"Ow!" the kitten said. "Ouch!
MeeOW!" but he kept struggling
upwards until...

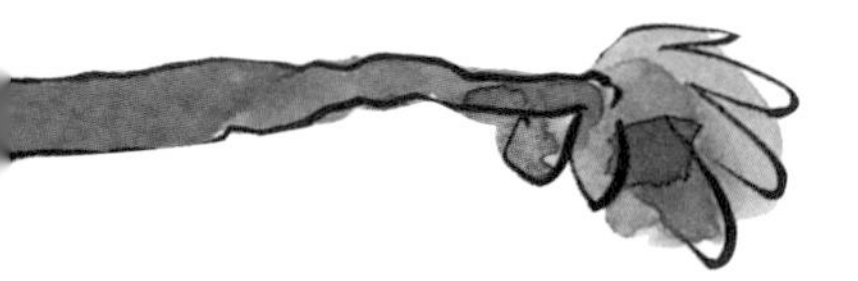

Pop!

Out he came at the top.
"Oh no!" said the voice, "you're a cat!
Now I'll be eaten and Father will be
furious!"
A big blue grey bird was lying flat on
his back in a neat little nest. His legs
were waving in the air, and he was
very definitely, stuck.
"Whatever are you doing?"
asked the kitten.
"I'm stuck!" said the bird crossly.
"I've been here for ages. Hurry up
and eat me."

"I don't want to eat you," said the kitten. "I came to help you."

"Are you sure?" The bird sounded surprised.

"Yes," the kitten said. "What can I do?"

The bird waved his legs again. "Pull me out, of course," he said.

The kitten balanced on a branch, and took hold of one of the blue grey bird's scaly legs.

"I'll count to three," said the bird. "Ready? One – two – three – pull!"

The kitten pulled and heaved and...

Crash!

The bird shot out of the nest and he and the kitten tumbled to the ground. "Ouch!" said the kitten, and he rubbed his head. The bird began to strut about, shaking his feathers. "Coo!" he said. "Did you see me fly?"

"Er ... yes," said the kitten.
"Best flyer ever, that's me!" said the bird. "Cuckoo! Cuckoo! Cuckoo bird. Pleased to meet you. I'd better go and find my mum and dad!"

"Yes," said the kitten sadly.

The cuckoo peered at the kitten with his beady black eyes. "Hey – what's up with you?"

"I'm looking for my mother," said the kitten. "I'm just not sure which way to go."

The cuckoo hopped up onto a twig. "Why didn't you say? I'll find her for you! Cuckoo! I can see everything from up in the air! What does she look like?"

"Like me," said the kitten. "Stripy with white paws. And she's got a white tip to her tail. Just like me."

"Easy!" said the cuckoo. "You wait here. I'll have a fly around and be back in no time."

"Thank you," said the kitten.

Cuckoo bird hopped higher up the hedge. "See you soon," he said.

"Here I go!
Cuckoo!"

The kitten watched until the cuckoo was a small speck, and then he curled up in the dead leaves.

"I hope he finds Mother soon,"
he thought. "I miss her so much.
But maybe she's found the very
special place for us to live where we'll
be loved and hugged …"
And the kitten began to dream
a happy dream.

Chapter Seven

The kitten woke up with a jump. He hadn't really meant to go to sleep. Where was the cuckoo? Surely he should have come back by now?

The kitten stared up into the sky,
but all he could see were
white fluffy clouds.

"Cuckoo! Cuckoo! Cuckoo!"

The cuckoo landed beside him
with a thump.

"Coo! Did you see that landing?"

The cuckoo was looking
very pleased with himself.

"Yes," said the kitten. "It was very clever indeed ... excuse me, but did you see my mother?"

"What? Oh, yes. She's not far away. She was sitting on a wall in front of a house, a big place."

The kitten was very excited. "You saw my mother? Are you sure? Did you tell her I was coming?"

The cuckoo took a step backwards.
“Certainly looked like you. White paws.”

“Oh – yes! Yes! That’s my mother!”
The kitten was trembling all over.
“Did you talk to her?”

"Didn't like to go bothering her," said the cuckoo. "She was being stroked by one of those humans."

"Wait!" The kitten ran after the cuckoo. "I can't fly!"

"Don't worry, little four paws," said the cuckoo. "Just keep your peepers open and shout if you get left behind."

With a swoop and a swerve and a dip and a dive the cuckoo was up in the air. "Cuckoo! Here we go!" he called.

The cuckoo flew above him shouting, "Keep going, little four paws!" but it was a long, hard journey.

When the kitten finally saw a wooden fence in front of him he gave a faint "Mew!" and collapsed in a heap. "I want my mother!" he said, and two huge tears rolled down his nose.

The cuckoo flew over the fence and round to the steps by the big house, where two children were making a fuss of a big cat with white paws.

"Cuckoo!" shouted the cuckoo at the top of his voice.

"Mew!" whispered the kitten. "Mew!"

"Poor little thing!" said a voice, and the kitten was scooped up.

"Put him in a basket," said another voice. "Fat Freda'll look after him."

The kitten was gently put down somewhere very soft…and then he heard the most wonderful sound in the whole, wide world.

He heard purring, and the purring was coming closer.

"Mother!" whispered the kitten.

And as a long, pink tongue began to lick him clean he gave a little happy sigh and went to sleep.

Chapter Eight

The kitten with no name was warm and cosy and comfortable. He wasn't in the fields. He wasn't under a gorse bush. He wasn't in a rabbit burrow. He was tucked up in a fluffy rug, and he could hear a steady purring from the other side of the basket.

"There's Mother," he thought sleepily, and he opened his eyes. "Good morning, my dear," said a big cat with white paws.

For a moment the kitten could say nothing at all. It looked like his mother. But it wasn't his mother. "Meeow!" said the kitten. "Who are you? Where's my mother?"

The cat didn't answer. She lifted the kitten out of the basket and dropped him down beside a saucer. "Breakfast," she said.

The smell of food was wonderful. The kitten ate and ate, and when he couldn't manage any more he stopped and licked his whiskers.

The big cat was cleaning her paws, "P'rrrrr. You'll feel better now," she said. "I'm Fat Freda. Have you come to live here? I thought you were the new kitten."

The kitten sighed. "I'm lost," he said sadly.
"Lost?" Fat Freda said. "You poor little thing."

The kitten told Fat Freda how he had
walked all the way from his house
under the hedge.
"The mouse and the frog and
the rabbit and the cuckoo all tried
to help me," he said, "but I don't think
I'll ever find my mother."

Fat Freda stood up and stretched.
"What did you say your mother
looked like?"
"Like me," said the kitten.
He looked at Fat Freda. "And like you."

"Fancy that," said Fat Freda. "Kitty Purr looks just like that. She lives at the top of the house with Granny Annie. Well, she used to, but she went away. Meeow! I've had an idea."

Then Fat Freda said, "You curl up here and have a rest, I'll be back soon." The kitten watched the big cat stroll out of the kitchen. It seemed very big and empty now he was on his own.

"Woof!
Woof woof woof!
Woof! Woof
woof woof!"
"Yap! Yap yap
yap yap!"

The kitten froze. The barking was getting nearer. He ran across the carpet as a huge monster dog and a small hairy dog dashed in. A rush of children and grown-ups with parcels and packages came after them.

The kitten leapt behind the squashy old sofa. He saw a little pink basket hanging on the radiator and dived inside.

The noises gradually settled down. The children chatted and laughed, and the kitten listened to what was going on.

"Is Granny Annie coming down for tea?" asked a voice.

"No, she's too sad," someone answered. "She walked down to the shops to see if anyone had seen Kitty Purr, but nobody had."

"Daisy B's got a pretty kitty," said a squeaky little voice. "Granny Annie can play with my kitty."

The kitten's ears twitched.
A long time ago a boy and a little girl had found him playing by his hedge, and the little girl had wanted to take him home. Was this her house? The kitten's ears drooped.
He sank down in the little pink basket.
What was going to happen to him?
What was he going to do?

"Kitty! There's my kitty!"
There was a loud clatter in the kitchen.
"Oh." Daisy B was nearly crying.
"Isn't my kitty. Is big cat!"

There was a sudden silence.
There was a meow, and then another.
A cat was calling to the kitten …

The kitten froze.

Then he leapt out of
the little pink basket.

"Mother!"

And this time it really
was his mother.

She sprang towards him and licked
him and purred and rolled him over
and over with her paw.
All the people in the kitchen laughed
and cheered and clapped their hands.

The kitchen door opened, and Granny Annie came hurrying in. The kitten's mother ran to her and wound round her legs, purring loudly.

For a second the kitten felt lonely. Then Daisy B picked him up. She hugged him and she hugged him, and it wasn't too tight. It was exactly the right sort of hug.

And that's how the kitten found
his home.

Did he find his name?
Oh yes...Daisy B called him Tiger,
but sometimes he was Pretty Kitty
or Fluffy Paws.

The kitten didn't mind.
He'd found his very special home
where he could live happily ever after.